STICKER STORIES

The Very First Christmas

illustrated by Elise Mills

Grosset & Dunlap
An Imprint of Penguin Group (USA) Inc.

ISBN 978-0-448-42867-3   20 19 18 17 16 15 14 13 12

Long ago, there lived a young woman named Mary. One day, an angel appeared to Mary. The angel told her that she was going to give birth to a baby boy.

Use the stickers to put Mary and the angel in the picture.

Just before the baby was born, Mary and her husband Joseph traveled to Bethlehem. When they arrived in the little town, there was no room at the inn. The innkeeper told Mary and Joseph they could sleep in his stable.

Use the stickers to fill in the town.

That very night, Mary's baby was born.
His name was Jesus. All the animals
gathered around the newborn baby.
A bright star twinkled in the sky above.

Use the stickers to surround
the baby Jesus with animals.

On a nearby hill, shepherds were watching over their sheep.
Suddenly, an angel appeared and told them the Son of God
had been born. At first, the shepherds were frightened.
But they decided to follow the star and find the baby Jesus.

Use the stickers to put
the shepherds in the scene.

When the shepherds reached the stable in Bethlehem,
their hearts filled with joy as they knelt beside the sleeping baby.

Fill the stable with stickers
of the shepherds visiting Jesus.

Far away to the east, three wise men saw a blazing star in the sky. They knew this meant a great king had been born. So they, too, followed the star to Bethlehem.

Use the stickers to add the wise
men and lots of stars to the picture.

13

The three wise men knelt beside Jesus and presented him with gifts.
"Behold, the Son of God," they all said.

What did the wise men give to Jesus?
Use the stickers to show what they brought.

The sweet song of angels filled the night air.
The baby Jesus looked up and smiled.
Everyone had come to celebrate his birthday—
the very first Christmas!

Fill in the picture with stickers to show
the joy of the first Christmas.